Farmyard Tales

The Hungry Donkey

Heather Amery

Illustrated by Stephen Cartwright

Adapted by Susanna Davidson
Reading consultant: Alison Kelly

 Find the duck on every double page.

This story is about Apple Tree Farm,

Poppy,   Sam,

Mrs.
Boot,

Mrs.
Rose

and Ears,
the donkey.

Ears, the donkey, lived
at Apple Tree Farm.

Today, she was
going out.

She was going to
a show.

Mrs. Boot put her in
a little cart.

Poppy and Sam
climbed in.

Off they went.

Mrs. Boot tied Ears to
a fence.

Ears didn't like it. She pulled at the rope.

Ears was free! She was also hungry...

"Yum," thought Ears.
"Flowers and fruit."

11

Ears took a big bite.

"Oh no!" cried Mrs. Rose. "My hat!"

Ears ran away.
Everyone chased her.

"Catch that naughty
donkey!" they cried.

At last, Ears stopped.

"I'm so sorry," said
Mrs. Boot.

"Would you like a ride in the donkey cart?"

Mrs. Rose rode the cart in the donkey show.

This time, Ears was
very good. She won
a prize.

Mrs. Rose won a prize too. It was a hat.

It was time to go. "That was fun," said Poppy.

Goodbye!

"Mrs. Rose has a new hat. And Ears has a new hat too."

PUZZLES

Puzzle 1

Put these pictures in the right order to tell the story.

A.

B.

C.

D.

E.

Puzzle 2

Who's who? Match the names
to the people or animals in
this story.

Sam

Poppy

Mrs. Boot

Mrs. Rose

Ears

Puzzle 3

Can you spot five differences between these two pictures?

Puzzle 4

Choose the right sentence for each picture.

A.

Mrs. Boot tied Ears to a fence.

Mrs. Boot tied Ears to a tree.

B.

Ears took a big biscuit.

Ears took a big bite.

C.

Everyone chose her.
Everyone chased her.

D.

"Naughty donkey," said Sam.
"Good donkey," said Sam.

Answers to puzzles
Puzzle 1

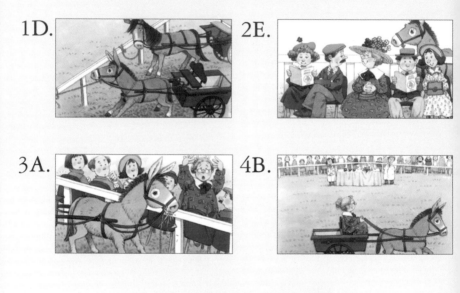

1D.

2E.

3A.

4B.

5C.

Puzzle 2

Ears

Mrs. Rose

Poppy

Mrs. Boot

Sam

Puzzle 3

Puzzle 4

A. Mrs. Boot
tied Ears
to a fence.

B. Ears took
a big bite.

C. Everyone
chased her.

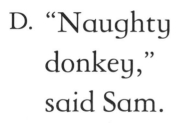

D. "Naughty
donkey,"
said Sam.

Designed by Laura Nelson
Series editor: Lesley Sims
Series designer: Russell Punter
Digital manipulation by John Russell

This edition first published in 2016 by Usborne Publishing Ltd.,
Usborne House, 83-85 Saffron Hill, London EC1N 8RT, England.
www.usborne.com Copyright © 2016, 1990 Usborne Publishing Ltd.